W9-CHO-716

STORM AT THE JETTY

STORM
AT THE JETTY

LEONARD EVERETT FISHER

The Viking Press, New York

First Edition/Copyright © Leonard Everett Fisher, 1981/All rights reserved/First published
in 1981 by The Viking Press, 625 Madison Avenue, New York, New York 10022/Published
simultaneously in Canada by Penguin Books Canada Limited/Printed in U.S.A.
1 2 3 4 5 85 84 83 82 81

Library of Congress Cataloging in Publication Data/Fisher, Leonard Everett. Storm at the
jetty./Summary: Levi watches a violent thunderstorm from his favorite place on the jetty.
[1. Thunderstorms—Fiction. 2. Seashore—Fiction] I. Title. PZ7.F533St
[E]   80-24402   ISBN 0-670-67214-9

The sea! the sea! the open sea!
The blue, the fresh, the ever free!

Bryan Waller Procter (1787-1874)

Low tide and daylight were Levi Farber's tide and time. The jetty was his place. There he sat, in the cockpit of the rocks, watching a lone ship and the rolling sea.

Most people who lived near the jetty were too busy to listen
to the sounds of the sea, the endless beat of the breaking
surf slapping the rocks or crashing into the seawall.

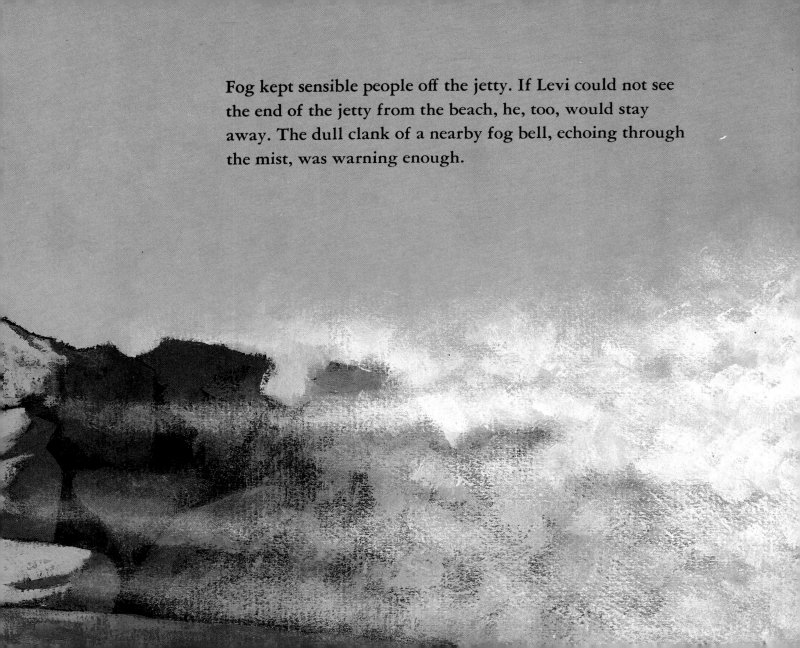

Fog kept sensible people off the jetty. If Levi could not see the end of the jetty from the beach, he, too, would stay away. The dull clank of a nearby fog bell, echoing through the mist, was warning enough.

Now, at noon, there was little sun in the gloomy sky. Summer was playing itself out. School was a week off. Usually the clear, dry days of August were hints of the coming fall. But not now. Now it was too dark for noon, and it was the wrong season for a storm brewing in the southwest.

A breeze began to push the clammy air from one side of the bay to the other. In minutes, choppy waves hammered the seawall with foamy spray. A complaining gull challenged the wind and lost. Its succulent dinner of silvery shiners below would have to wait.

Levi, his eyes smarting from the wind-whipped brine,
saw fingers of lightning jab the distant beach. Behind him,
a rusty crab darted out of a shadowy crevice, looking
for a better place to hide.

The sea heaved, twisted, and smashed into the jetty. A gust of wind pushed Levi against the slippery rocks. The fog bell clanked as a foggy squall rapidly approached. Thunder growled and rolled inland. Day became night at noontime. It was time to leave the jetty—quickly!

Another blast of thunder shattered the air. The whirling mist disappeared, chased by the wind and driving rain. Levi, soaked from the rain and the spray, fled up the seawall ladder to safety.

Behind the rain-streaked window of the big house, Levi, dripping and breathless, stared at another crackling line of lightning. It leaped out of the watery blackness above and slammed into the lighthouse roof. The rain in its wake became steam.

For a moment the jetty glowed eerily in the white-hot light.
Beyond, more lightning stabbed the ghostly silhouette of a
great ship reaching for the open sea.

Suddenly the rain stopped and the air began to clear. Levi could see the jetty again. Windowpanes shook slightly with every diminishing rumble of thunder. Levi watched the storm move northeast—away. Soon a startling quiet invaded the sea.

The sun broke through, spreading its warming heat over the water. Silent and spent from its wild struggle, the sea rested.

The jetty stood, firm as always, bathed in the brightness of the clear afternoon. Levi climbed onto the rocks. Now he could sit on the jetty's point, in the cockpit of the rocks, once again.

About the Jetty

The jetty actually exists—at the foot of Beach 48th Street in Sea Gate, a small community in Brooklyn, New York. About fifty yards long—half a football field—the seventy-five-year-old breakwater, now fast sinking, pokes westward toward Staten Island. The house shown in this book is the author's boyhood home.

About the Art

The illustrations for this book were painted in six tones of gray acrylics plus black and white. The art was photographed, then printed in duotones of blue and black ink. The text typeface is Linotype Garamond Bold Number 3; the display typeface is Typositor Augustea Inline.

About the Author

Leonard Everett Fisher, illustrator of more than two hundred books, author of thirty-five, received the 1979 Medallion of the University of Southern Mississippi for "distinguished contributions to children's literature."

Mr. Fisher, a resident of Connecticut, is also a noted painter and designer of postage stamps. In 1950 he received the Pulitzer Painting Award. His work is included in museum collections all over the United States.